Rosy's Journey

and other stories

Miles Kelly

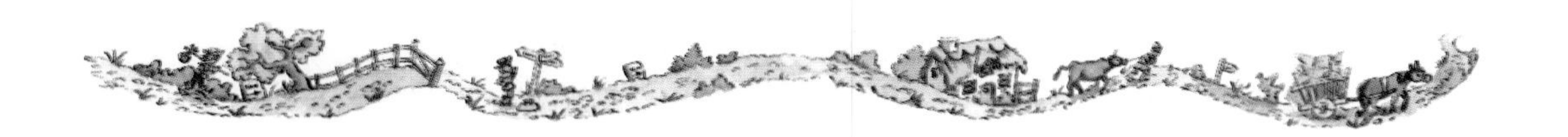

First published in 2011 by Miles Kelly Publishing Ltd
Harding's Barn, Bardfield End Green, Thaxted, Essex, CM6 3PX, UK

This edition printed in 2013

2 4 6 8 10 9 7 5 3 1

Publishing Director Belinda Gallagher
Creative Director Jo Cowan
Editor Amanda Askew
Senior Designer Joe Jones
Designer Kayleigh Allen
Production Manager Elizabeth Collins
Reprographics Anthony Cambray, Stephan Davis, Jennifer Hunt
Assets Lorraine King

ISBN 978-1-78209-277-3

Printed in China

British Library Cataloguing-in-Publication Data
A catalogue record for this book is available from the British Library

ACKNOWLEDGMENTS
Artworks are from the Miles Kelly Artwork Bank

Made with paper from a sustainable forest

www.mileskelly.net
info@mileskelly.net

www.factsforprojects.com

Contents

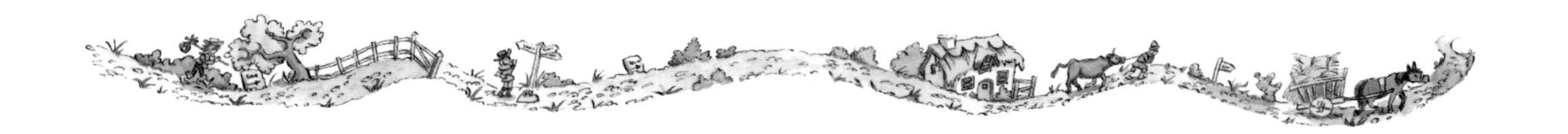

The Precious Stove

An Austrian folk tale

Peter lived with his mother, father, brothers, and sisters in an old wooden cottage, deep in the woods of Austria. They were very poor and the cottage had hardly any furniture, and they might have been very cold in winter were it not for their most treasured possession, a stove. This was no ordinary stove. It was made of white porcelain and it was so tall, the gold crown at the top almost scraped the ceiling. Its feet were carved like lion's

claws, the talons painted gold. The sides of the stove were painted with flowers and rare birds, in glowing colors, and the door was tiled in blue and gold. It looked very out of place in the poor wooden cottage, for it had originally been made for a king's palace. Many years before, Peter's grandfather had rescued it, after a great war, from the ruins of the palace where he used to work. Peter used to draw copies of the flowers and birds on pieces of brown paper with a stub of old pencil.

One evening, as Peter and his sister Gilda lay curled up in the warmth at the foot of the stove, their father came in, shaking the snow from his boots. He looked tired and ill.

"My children, tomorrow the stove will be taken away as I have had to sell it. We have no money, and we need food more than we need a stove."

The children were horrified, but their father would not change his mind. That night, instead of banking up the stove to keep it burning warmly through the night, he let the fire die down so it was quite cold in the morning. The traders arrived and loaded the stove onto a cart. Peter's mother and father looked at the handful of gold coins the traders had given them and shook their heads.

Peter and Gilda whispered together outside behind the wood pile.

"You have to follow the cart, Peter," said Gilda, "so you can see where our stove goes."

So Peter rushed off down the track after the cart, pausing only to grab a couple of apples. The journey into town was slow, but by evening it had

reached the station. Peter crept as close as he dared, and heard the traders arranging for the stove to go to Vienna by train the very next morning. Once the traders had gone to an inn for the night, he clambered inside the stove. He soon fell fast asleep.

When he awoke, the train was moving fast. Peter munched his apples and wondered what his parents would be thinking, just where was he going to end up, and what could he do to keep the stove for his family.

Eventually the train came to a halt and with much banging and clattering all the boxes around the stove were unloaded onto the platform. Then Peter heard a gruff voice.

"That valuable stove is going to the palace. Take care it isn't damaged in any way."

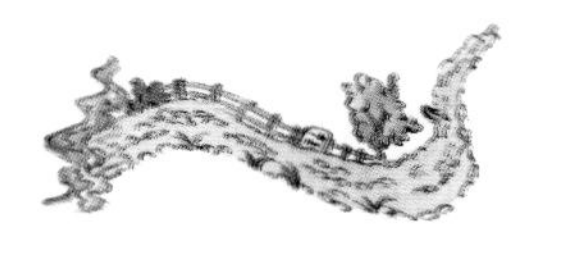

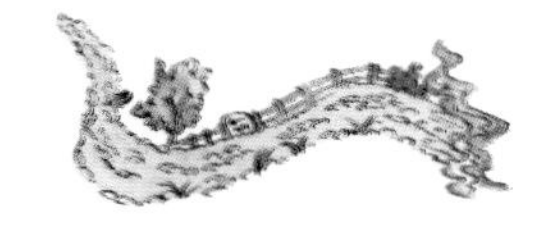

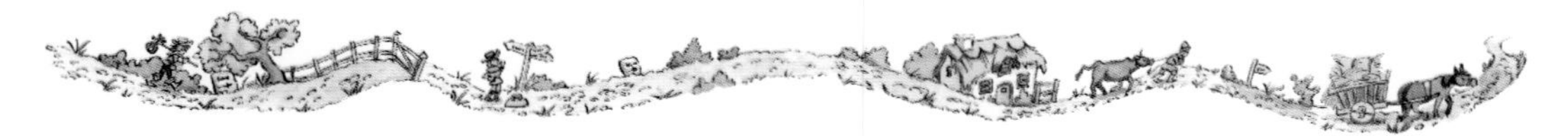

The palace! Peter sat as quiet as a mouse as he felt the stove lifted onto another cart. It clattered through cobbled streets and then came to a halt.

"Truly, it is a very beautiful stove. I did not expect it to be so fine," said a deep important voice. And then the handle of the door turned and light flooded into the stove. Peter tumbled out onto the floor, before looking up at a man dressed in a bright red jacket with great gold tassels and gold buttons. Glittering medals gleamed on his chest and a great silver sword hung by his side. It was the king! Peter was absolutely terrified, but the king kept on smiling.

"Well, my boy, how did you come to be inside my new stove?"

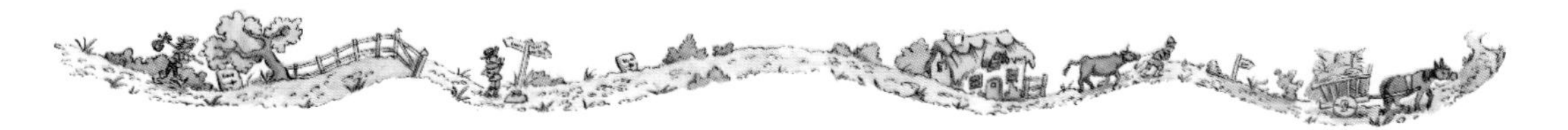

A servant rushed forward and grabbed Peter by the arm, meaning to drag him away, but the king raised his hand and the man stepped back.

"Let the child speak," said the king.

Well, once Peter found his tongue, he could not stop. He told the king all about the stove. The king listened in silence while Peter told his story.

"Peter, I am not going to give you back your stove for it belongs here in the palace, but I will give your father several bags of gold, for it is a very valuable stove. And perhaps you would like to stay here and look after it for me?" he asked.

Peter was delighted. And he looked after the stove for the king from that day on. His family never wanted for food again, and every summer they would all come to stay at the palace to see Peter—and the stove of course.

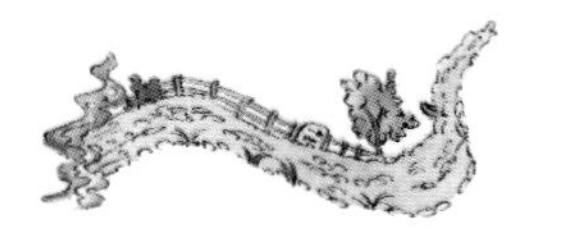

The Three Sillies

By Joseph Jacobs

Once upon a time, there was a farmer and his wife who had one daughter. She was to marry a gentleman. Every evening, the gentleman had supper at the farmhouse, and the daughter went down into the cellar to fetch the beer for him.

One evening she went down to fetch the beer, when she looked up at the ceiling and saw a mallet stuck in one of the beams. She thought it was very dangerous to have that mallet there, and said to

herself, "Suppose him and me were to be married, and we were to have a son, and he was to grow up to be a man, and come down into the cellar to get the beer and the mallet was to fall on his head and kill him!" And she started crying.

Upstairs, they began to wonder why it was taking her so long, so her mother went down to the cellar. She found her daughter crying, with the beer running over the floor. "Whatever is the matter?" said her mother.

"Oh, mother!" said she, "look at that horrid mallet! Suppose we were to be married, and were to have a son, and he was to grow up, and was to come down to the cellar to fetch the beer, and the mallet was to fall on his head and kill him!"

"Dear, dear!" said the mother, and she started crying too. Then after a bit the father began to wonder why they hadn't come back, and he went

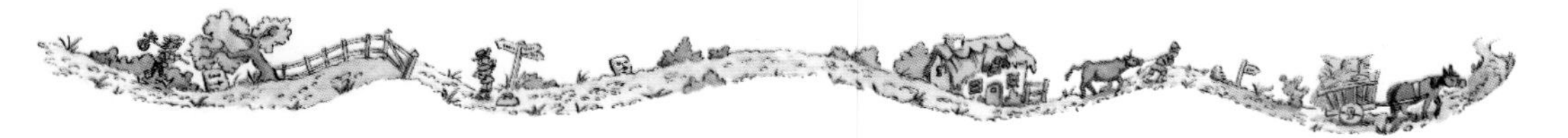

down into the cellar to look for them. There the two sat crying, with the beer running all over the floor. "Whatever is the matter?" said he.

"Why," said the mother, "look at that horrid mallet. Just suppose, if our daughter and her sweetheart were to be married, and were to have a son, and he was to grow up, and was to come down into the cellar to fetch the beer, and the mallet was to fall on his head and kill him!"

"Dear, dear!" said the father, and he sat down beside the other two, and started crying.

Now the gentleman got tired of being in the kitchen by himself, and at last he went down into the cellar to see what they were doing. There the three sat crying, with the beer running all over the floor. He turned off the tap and asked, "Whatever are you three doing, sitting crying, and letting the beer run all over the floor?"

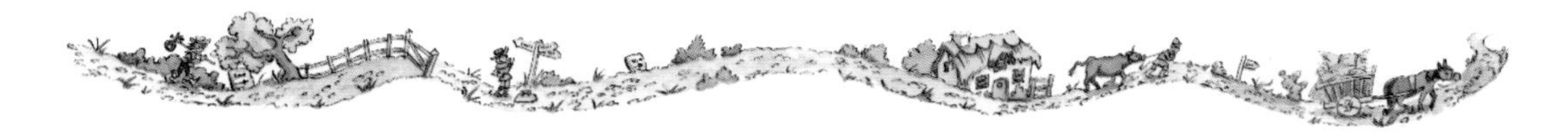

"Oh!" said the father, "look at that horrid mallet! Suppose you and our daughter were to be married, and were to have a son, and he was to grow up, and come down into the cellar to fetch the beer, and the mallet was to fall on his head and kill him!"

And then they all started crying worse than before. But the gentleman burst out laughing, and reached up, pulled out the mallet, and said, "I've traveled many miles, and I've never met three such

sillies before. Now I shall start out on my travels again, and if I can find three bigger sillies, then I'll come back and marry your daughter." So he wished them goodbye, and went on his travels.

First, he came to a woman's cottage that had some grass growing on the roof. The woman was trying to get her cow to go up a ladder. The gentleman asked the woman what she was doing.

"Look at all that beautiful grass. I'm going to get the cow on to the roof to eat it. She'll be safe, for I shall tie a string round her neck, and pass it down the chimney, and tie it to my wrist, so she can't fall off without my knowing."

"Oh, you poor silly!" said the gentleman, "you should cut the grass and throw it to the cow!" But the woman thought it was easier to get the cow up the ladder than to get the grass down.

The gentleman went on his way, but he hadn't

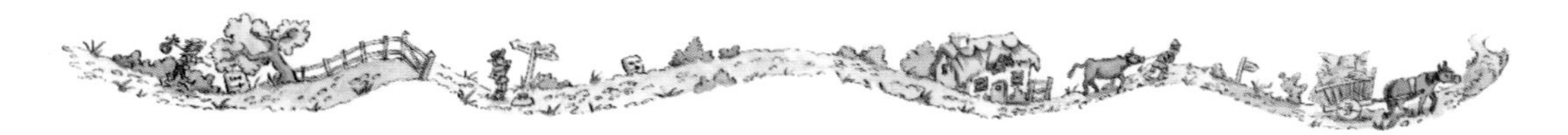

gone far when the cow tumbled off the roof and the weight of the cow pulled the woman up the chimney, where she got stuck, covered in soot. Well, that was one big silly.

The gentleman went on, and stopped the night at an inn, but it was so full that he had to share a room. In the morning, the gentleman was surprised to see the other man hang his pants on the chest of drawers, run across the room and try to jump into them. At last he stopped. "Oh dear," he said, "It takes me an hour to get into my pants every morning. How do you manage yours?" The gentleman burst out laughing, and showed him how to put them on. He said that he never would have thought of doing it that way. So that was another big silly.

Then the gentleman went on his travels again, and he came to a village, where there was a crowd of people around a pond. They had rakes and brooms, reaching into the pond. The gentleman asked what was the matter.

"Why," they said, "the moon's tumbled into the pond, and we can't get her out!" So the gentleman burst out laughing, and told them to look into the sky, and that it was only the shadow in the water.

So there were a whole lot of sillies bigger than those three sillies at home. So the gentleman turned back home again and married the farmer's daughter.

The Two Frogs

By Andrew Lang

Once upon a time in the country of Japan there lived two frogs, one of whom made his home in a ditch near the town of Osaka, on the sea coast, while the other dwelt in a clear little stream that ran through the city of Kyoto.

They had never heard of each other, but, funnily enough, the idea came into both their heads at once that they should like to see the world, and the frog who lived at Kyoto wanted to visit Osaka, and

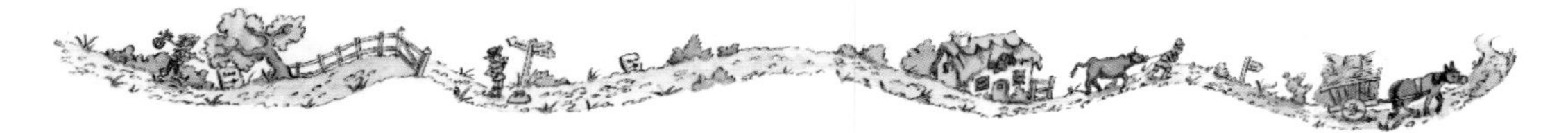

the frog who lived at Osaka wished to go to Kyoto.

So one fine morning, they both set out along the road that led from Kyoto to Osaka, one from one end and the other from the other. Halfway between the two towns there arose a mountain that had to be climbed. It took them a long time and a great many hops to reach the top, but there they were at last, and what was the surprise of each to see another frog before him!

They looked at each other for a moment without speaking, and then told each other why they were there. It was delightful to find that they both wanted to learn a little more of their country.

"What a pity we are not bigger," said the Osaka frog, "then we could see both towns from here, and tell if it is worth our while going on."

"Oh, that's easy," said the Kyoto frog. "We have only got to stand up on our hind legs, hold onto

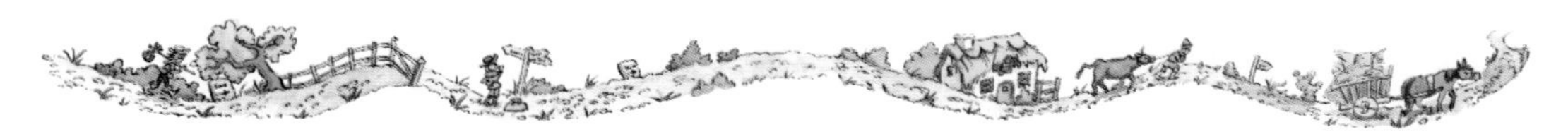

each other, and then we can look at the towns."

This idea pleased the Osaka frog so much that he at once jumped up and put his front paws on the shoulder of his friend, who had risen also. There they both stood, stretching themselves as high as they could, and holding each other tightly, so that they might not fall down.

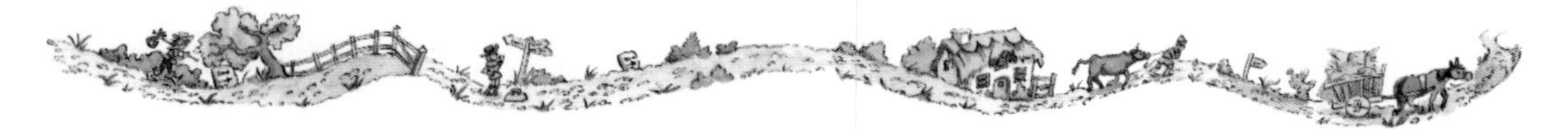

The Kyoto frog turned his nose toward Osaka, and the Osaka frog turned his nose toward Kyoto. But they forgot that when they stood up, their eyes lay in the backs of their heads, so they looked behind them.

"Dear me!" cried the Osaka frog, "Kyoto is exactly like Osaka. It is certainly not worth such a long journey. I shall go home!"

"If I had had any idea that Osaka was only a copy of Kyoto I should never have traveled all this way," exclaimed the frog from Kyoto. As he spoke he took his hands from his friend's shoulders and they both fell down on the grass. Then they took a polite farewell of each other and set off for home again, and to the end of their lives they believed that Osaka and Kyoto, which are as different as two towns can be, were as alike as two peas in a pod.

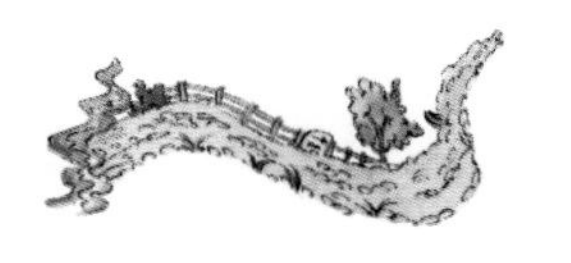

Honorable Minu

By William H Barker

One day, a poor man had to travel from his own little village to Accra—one of the big towns on the coast. This man could not speak their language, and they could not speak his.

As he approached Accra he met a great herd of cows. He was surprised at the number of them, and wondered who they belonged to. Seeing a man with them he asked, "Who do these cows belong to?" The man replied, "Minu," which

means I do not understand. The poor man, however, thought that Minu was the name of the owner of the cows and exclaimed, "Mr Minu must be very rich."

He then entered the town. Very soon he saw a fine large building, and wondered who it belonged to. The man he asked did not understand his question, so he also answered, "Minu."

"Dear me! What a rich fellow Mr Minu must be!" cried the poor man.

Coming to an even finer building with beautiful

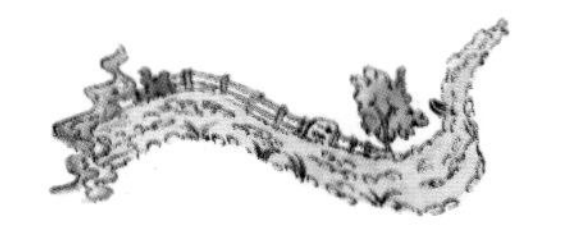

gardens round it, he again asked the owner's name. Again came the answer, "Minu."

"How wealthy Mr Minu is!" said the poor man.

Next he came to the beach. There he saw a magnificent steamer being loaded in the harbor. He asked, "Who does this fine vessel belong to?"

"Minu," replied the man.

"To the Honorable Minu also! He is the richest man I ever heard of!" cried the poor man.

Having finished his business, he set off for home. As he passed down one of the streets, he met men carrying a coffin. He asked the name of the dead person, and received the usual reply, "Minu."

"Poor Mr Minu!" he cried. "He has left all his wealth and died just as a poor person would do! In future, I will be happy with my tiny house and little money." And then he went home quite pleased.

Straw, Coal, and Bean

By the Brothers Grimm

An old woman lived in a village. She had gathered a serving of beans and wanted to cook them, so she prepared a fire in her fireplace. To make it burn faster she lit it with a handful of straw. While she was pouring the beans into the pot, one of them fell unnoticed to the floor, coming to rest next to a piece of straw. Soon afterward a glowing coal jumped out of the fireplace and landed next to them.

The straw said, "Friends, where do you come from?"

The coal answered, "I jumped from the fireplace. If I had not forced my way out, I would have died. I would have burned to ash."

The bean said, "I too saved my skin. If the old woman had gotten me into the pot I would have been cooked to mush."

"Would my fate have been any better?" said the straw. "The old woman sent all my brothers up in fire and smoke. She grabbed sixty at once and killed them. I slipped through her fingers."

"What should we do now?" asked the coal.

"Because we have so fortunately escaped death," answered the bean, "I think that we should join together as comrades. To prevent some new misfortune from befalling us here, let us together make our way to another land."

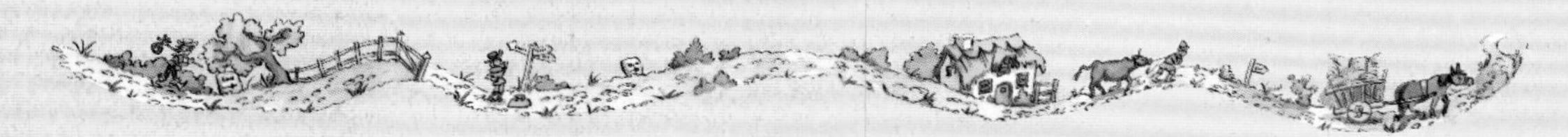

This pleased the other two, and they set off. They soon came to a small brook. The straw decided to lay across it, so the others could walk across him.

When the coal got to the middle, he stopped, scared to go any further. Then the straw caught fire and fell into the brook. The coal slid after him, hissing as he fell into the water.

The bean who had stayed on the bank laughed until he burst. A wandering tailor was there, resting near the brook. He got out a needle and thread and sewed the bean back together. The bean thanked him and because he used black thread, all beans now have a black seam.

Dick Whittington and his Cat

An English myth

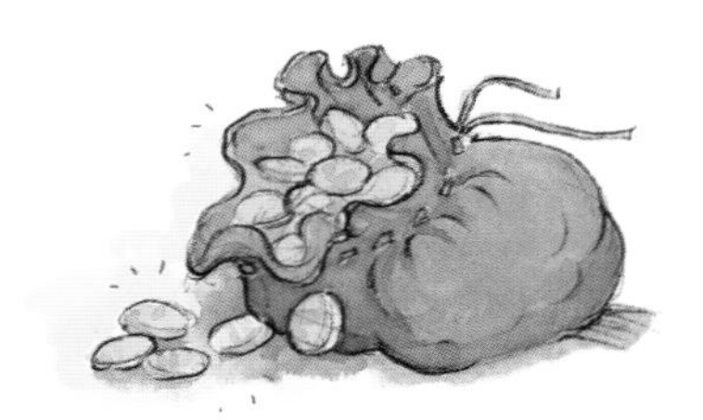

Hundreds of years ago there lived a poor orphan boy called Dick Whittington. His only possession was his cat, but everyone in his village looked after him, so he never wanted for a meal or clothes on his back. In return, he worked hard wherever he was needed. Now Dick's greatest dream was to visit the great city of London where, he had heard, the streets were paved with gold.

One day, a waggoner pulled into the village to

give his two horses a drink. Dick offered to rub the horses down, and before long he was telling the waggoner about his dreams of visiting London.

"Well, you must be in luck," smiled the waggoner, "for that is where I am bound. Why don't you come with me and I will drop you back here again tomorrow?"

This was too good an offer to refuse, so Dick and his cat set off with the waggoner for London. When they arrived, Dick looked round about in astonishment.

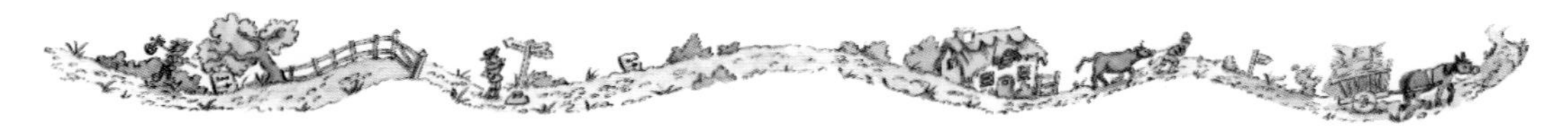

Never before had he seen such huge buildings, all crowded so closely together. And there were so many people! Dick set off to explore, promising the waggoner that he would be back in the evening.

The pavements certainly did not appear to be made of gold. But he kept on thinking he should just try round the next corner, and then the next and, before long, Dick realized that he was lost. He stumbled into a doorway, and worn out with hunger and worry, he fell asleep.

Now as luck would have it, Dick had chosen a very good doorway to sleep in. The house belonged to a rich merchant, Mr Fitzwarren, who was kind and willing to help anyone in need. So when he came home later that evening, Mr Fitzwarren took Dick and his cat indoors and told the cook to give him supper.

The next morning, Dick told Mr Fitzwarren the

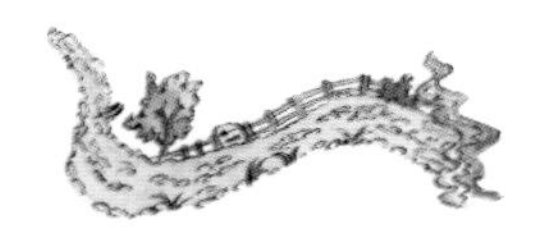

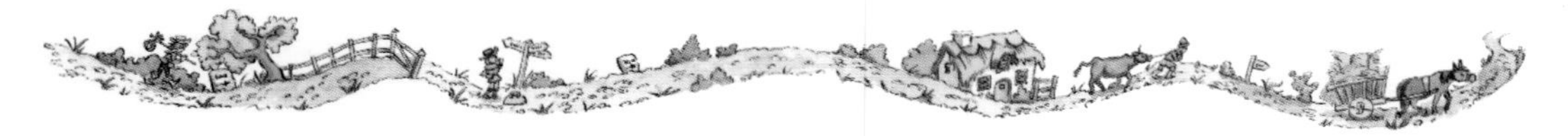

whole story. Smiling, Mr Fitzwarren told Dick that, as he had found, the streets of London were not paved with gold, and indeed life there was hard.

"But you look like a strong boy, would you like to work for me, Dick?" he asked. "You will have a roof over your head and dinner every day in return for helping in the kitchen and the stables."

Dick was delighted, and soon settled into the household. He worked hard, and everyone liked him, except the cook. She gave him all the horrible jobs in the kitchen and would not let him have a moment's rest.

Whenever one of Mr Fitzwarren's ships went to sea, it was custom for everyone in the household to give something to the ship's cargo for luck. Dick had only his cat. He sadly handed her over.

The ship was at sea for many months before they came to port in China. The captain and crew

went ashore to show the emperor their cargo. The emperor and captain sat down to a banquet before discussing business. But to the emperor's embarrassment, the meal was ruined by the rats that ran everywhere, even over the plates they were eating off. The emperor explained that they had tried everything but nothing could rid the court of the plague of rats. The captain smiled. "I think I have the answer," he said and he sent for Dick's cat. Within moments of her arrival, there were piles of dead rats at the emperor's feet. He was so impressed that he gave the captain a ship full of gold just for the cat.

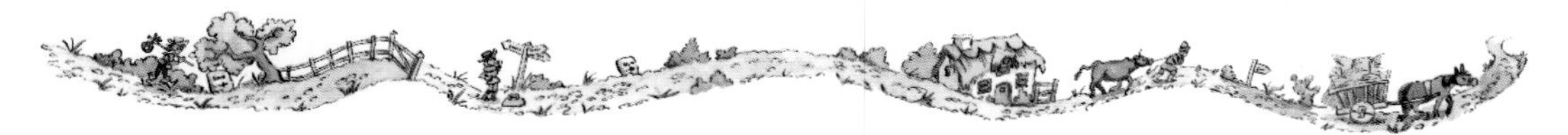

Back in London, Dick's life was a misery. The cook was nastier than ever and he didn't even have his beloved cat, so he ran away. But he had not gone far before he heard the church bells ringing, and they seemed to say, 'Turn again Dick Whittington, Thrice Lord Mayor of London.'

Dick didn't know what the bells meant, but he went back before the cook had even noticed that he was missing. Of course when the ships came home, Mr Fitzwarren gave Dick his fair share. He married Mr Fitzwarren's daughter, Jane, and became Lord Mayor of London three times. He and Jane had many children, and lots of cats!

Rosy's Journey

By Louisa May Alcott

Rosy was a girl who lived with her mother in a small house in the woods. They were very poor, for the father had gone away to dig for gold, and had not come back. When Rosy's mother died, she was left all alone, with no mother, no home, and no money. "What will you do?" said the people. "I will find my father," answered Rosy, bravely and days later, she started through the wood on a journey to find him.

One day, as she was resting by a river, she saw a fish on the bank, nearly dead for want of water.

"Poor thing! Go and be happy again," she said, taking him up, and dropping him into the river.

"Thank you, dear child, I'll not forget, but will help you some day," said the fish.

"Why, how can a tiny fish help such a great girl as I am?" laughed Rosy.

"Wait and see," answered the fish, as he swam away with a flap of his little tail.

Rosy went on her way, and forgot all about it. Soon after, as she was looking in the grass for strawberries, she found a field mouse with a broken leg. Rosy took the mouse carefully in her hand and tied up the broken leg with a leaf of spearmint and a blade of grass. Then she carried her to the nest under the roots of an old tree where four

baby mice were squeaking sadly for their mother. She made a bed of thistledown for the sick mouse, and put within close reach all the berries and seeds she could find, and brought an acorn-cup of water from the spring, so they could be comfortable.

"Good little Rosy, I shall pay you for all this kindness some day," said the mouse.

"I'm afraid you are not big enough to do much," answered Rosy, as she continued on her journey.

"Wait and see," called the mouse, and all the little ones squeaked as if they said the same.

Some time after, as Rosy lay up in a tree, waiting for the sun to rise, she heard a great buzzing close by and saw a fly caught in a cobweb. A big spider was trying to spin him up, and the poor fly was struggling to get away.

Rosy put up her finger and pulled down the web, and the spider ran away to hide. But the fly

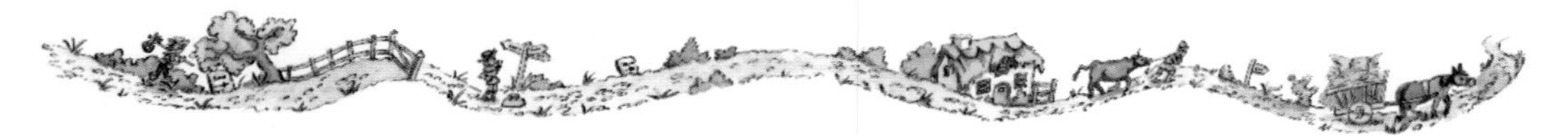

sat on Rosy's hand, cleaning his wings.

"You've saved my life, and I'll save yours, if I can," said the fly, twinkling his bright eye at Rosy.

"You silly thing, you can't help me," answered Rosy. The fly buzzed away, saying, like the mouse and fish, "Wait and see, wait and see."

Rosy trudged on, till at last she came to the sea. The mountains were on the other side, but how should she get over the water? She sat on the shore, tired and sad, and cried.

"Hello!" called a bubbly sort of voice close by, and the fish popped up his head.

"I've come to help you," said the fish. "I shall call my friend the whale and he will take you over."

Down dived the little fish, and Rosy waited to see what would happen, for she didn't believe such a tiny thing could really bring a whale to help her.

Presently what looked like a small island came

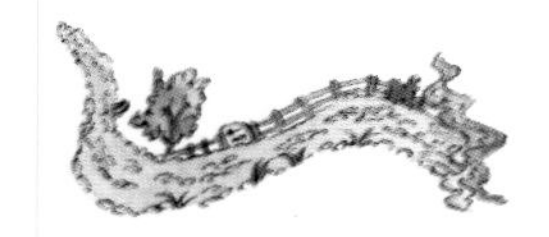

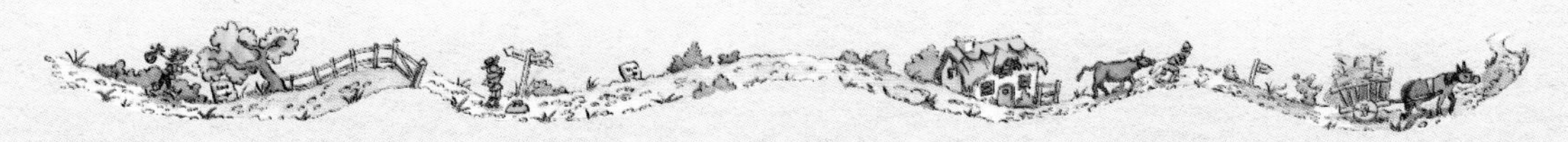

floating through the sea. Rosy was rather scared at this big, strange boat, but she got safely over, and held on fast. So she had a very pleasant voyage, and ran on shore with many thanks to the good whale, who gave a splendid spout and swam away.

Rosy traveled along till she came to a desert, hundreds of miles of hot sand.

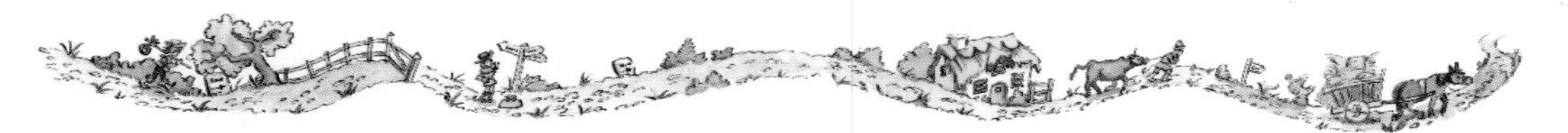

"I never can go that way," she said, "I should starve, and soon be worn out."

"Here I come to help you," said a friendly voice, and there was the mouse.

"Why, you dear little thing, I'm very glad to see you, but I'm sure you can't help me across this desert," said Rosy, stroking its soft back.

"That's easy," answered the mouse, rubbing its paws briskly. "I'll just call my friend the lion."

In a moment a loud roar was heard, and a splendid yellow lion, with fiery eyes and a long mane, came bounding over the sand. He crouched down like a great cat, and Rosy climbed up, and away they went, racing over the sand till her hair whistled in the wind. When they reached the other side, Rosy thanked the beast, and he ran away.

Rosy saw great hills before her, with many steep roads winding up to the top. She started off

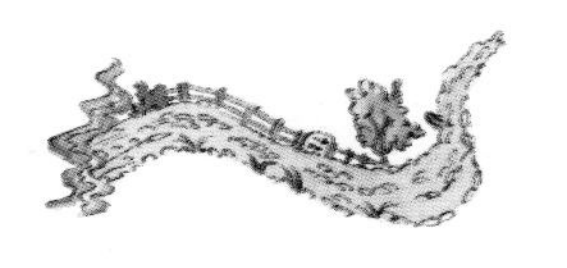

bravely, but took the wrong road, and after climbing a long while, she found the path ended in rocks over which she could not go. She was tired, hungry and cold. She lay down on the moss and cried a little, then she tried to sleep, but something kept buzzing in her ear. It was the fly.

"Rosy, don't cry—I'm here to help you all I can," said the fly. "My friend the eagle will carry you right up the mountains and leave you at your father's door."

When a great eagle swooped down and stopped near her, Rosy nestled into the thick brown feathers, and put both arms round his neck, and whiz they went, up, up, up, higher and higher, till

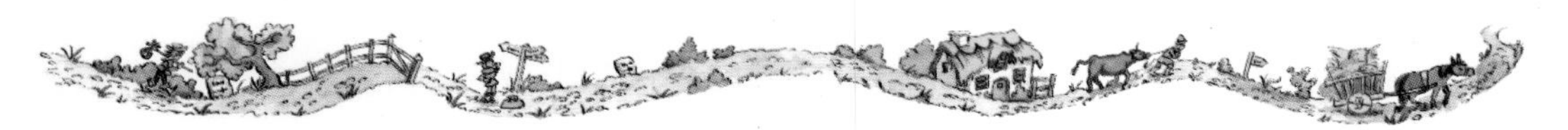

the trees looked like grass, they were so far below.

It was night when they landed, but fires were burning in all the houses, so Rosy went from hut to hut trying to find her father's. At last, in one hung a picture of a pretty little girl on the wall, and under it was written, "My Rosy."

Then she knew that this was the right place, and she ate some supper, put on more wood and went to bed, for she wanted to be fresh when her father came in the morning. She was finally home, ready to live happily with her father for the rest of their lives.